Lost and Found Pony

Do you love ponies? Be a Pony Pal!

Look for these Pony Pal books:

Lost and Found Pony

Jeanne Betancourt

Illustrated by Paul Bachem

SCHOLASTIC INC.
New York Toronto London Auckland Sydney
Mexico City New Delhi Hong Kong

ISBN 0-439-16572-5

12 11 10 9 8 7 6 5 4 3 2 1 1 2 3 4 5 6/0

Printed in the U.S.A.
First Scholastic printing, January 2001

Contents

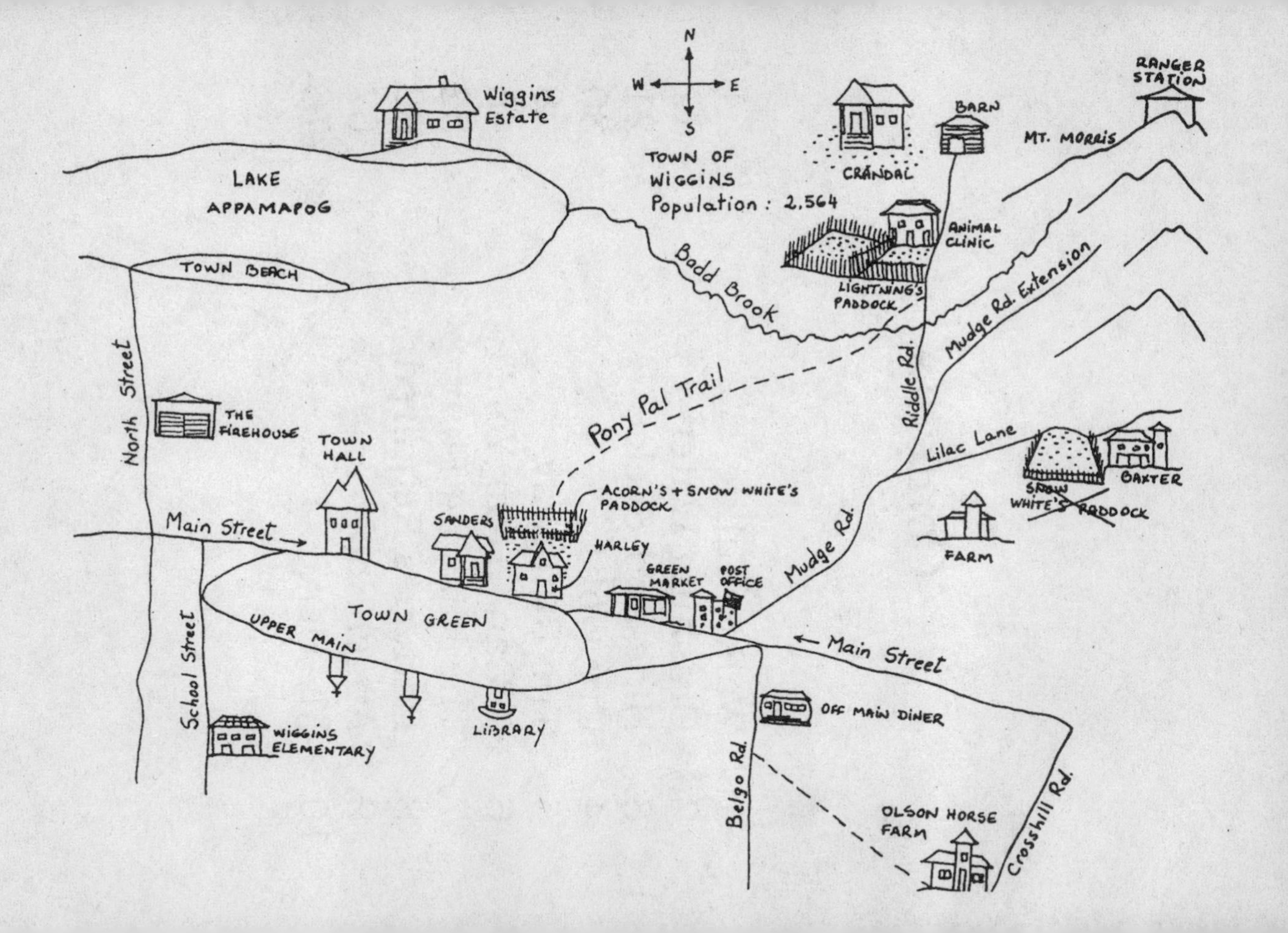
N
W
E
S
TOWN OF WIGGINS
Population : 2,564
Wiggins Estate
LAKE APPAMAPOG
TOWN BEACH
CRANDAL
BARN
RANGER STATION
MT. MORRIS
ANIMAL CLINIC
LIGHTNING'S PADDOCK
Badd Brook
Mudge Rd. Extension
Riddle Rd.
Pony Pal Trail
Lilac Lane
BAXTER
SNOW WHITE'S PADDOCK
FARM
North Street
THE FIREHOUSE
TOWN HALL
Main Street
SANDERS
ACORN'S + SNOW WHITE'S PADDOCK
HARLEY
GREEN MARKET
POST OFFICE
Mudge Rd.
TOWN GREEN
UPPER MAIN
Main Street
School Street
WIGGINS ELEMENTARY
LIBRARY
OFF MAIN DINER
Belgo Rd.
OLSON HORSE FARM
Crosshill Rd.

Walkie-Talkie

Anna brushed her pony's side with a hard brush. "We're going for a trail ride with our Pony Pals today," Anna told Acorn. Clumps of dirt fell from Acorn's hair. "You silly," said Anna. "You were rolling around in the dirt again."

Anna looked over at Lulu's pony, Snow White. Lulu and Anna were Pony Pals. Her pony, Snow White, and Acorn shared the paddock. There was a big blotch of dirt on Snow White, too. Anna smiled to herself. If one pony started to roll in the mud, the other one would copy.

Anna saw Lulu running across the paddock.

The two friends talked and laughed while they saddled their ponies for the trail ride. Soon Pam and Lightning would be there. It was Saturday and the Pony Pals were spending the whole day riding and picnicking on Ms. Wiggins's land. Ms. Wiggins kept her trails in good shape and there were beautiful spots for picnicking. Especially near Badd Brook.

"Look out, here comes Rosalie," Lulu told Anna. "She probably wants a pony ride."

Six-year-old Rosalie Lacey scooted under the fence and ran toward the two girls and their ponies. She was talking the whole time.

"We can't hear you," Anna shouted to Rosalie.

As Rosalie came closer, Anna saw that she wasn't talking to them. She was speaking into a bright blue walkie-talkie.

"Okay, I'm in their paddock," Rosalie said

into the walkie-talkie. "Can you still hear me?"

Rosalie held the walkie-talkie to her ear and listened for a few seconds. She was grinning from ear to ear. "It still works," she told Anna and Lulu. "I'm across the street and it still works."

"That's great," said Anna.

Anna wondered who was on the other end. She hoped it wasn't Rosalie's older brother, Mike. The Pony Pals liked Rosalie Lacey, but they didn't like Mike that much. He and his friend Tommy Rand were always making trouble.

Rosalie handed the walkie-talkie to Anna. "Listen," she told Anna.

A little girl's voice came over the walkie-talkie. "Can you *still* hear me?" she asked.

Anna recognized the voice of five-year-old Mimi Kline.

"Hi, Mimi," Anna said into the walkie-talkie. "This is Anna. I'm in Acorn's paddock and I can hear you loud and clear all the way from your house."

"I'm not in my house anymore," Mimi told Anna. "I'm in the woods now. Can you still hear me?"

"I can," said Anna. "But you shouldn't be in the woods alone. Remember? Is Mrs. Bell baby-sitting for you today?"

"Uh-huh," said Mimi.

"And does she know where you are?" asked Anna.

"Can you still hear me?" Mimi asked back. "I'm far away now."

Anna sighed. Mimi could be a lot of trouble, just like her little Shetland pony, Tongo.

"Mimi," said Anna. "Go back to your own yard or we won't talk to you."

"Okay, okay," said Mimi over the walkie-talkie.

Anna handed the walkie-talkie back to Rosalie.

While Rosalie talked to Mimi on the walkie-talkie, Anna and Lulu finished saddling up their ponies.

"Here come Pam and Lightning," Rosalie told Mimi. "I think the Pony Pals are going for a trail ride." Rosalie listened while Mimi said something back.

"Okay," Rosalie told Mimi. "I'm going to ask them."

Anna and Lulu exchanged a glance. They already knew what Rosalie and Mimi would ask.

"Can Mimi and Tongo and I go on the trail ride with you?" Rosalie asked the Pony Pals. "I don't have to ride. I'll run next to you." She kissed Acorn's cheek. "And maybe I can have a *little* ride on Acorn some of the time. *Please* can we come with you?"

Anna felt sorry for Rosalie. She loved ponies with all her heart, but she didn't have one. Her mother didn't like animals so Rosalie couldn't have any pets.

"Please, please, please!" shouted Mimi over the walkie-talkie.

The Pony Pals exchanged a glance. It was hard to say no to Rosalie and Mimi.

"Okay," Pam told Rosalie. "But only for a short ride on Pony Pal Trail." Pony Pal Trail was a mile-and-a-half trail through the woods. It connected Pam's place with Acorn and Snow White's paddock.

"Rosalie, you can ride Acorn the whole time," said Anna.

"But after the ride we're bringing you back to Mimi's," said Lulu, "because then we're going on a longer ride by ourselves."

"Are you going to have a picnic on the long ride?" asked Rosalie.

"Yes," answered Anna.

"They're going to have a picnic, too," Rosalie told Mimi over the walkie-talkie. "But they said we can't go on that."

While Rosalie listened to Mimi's answer, Pam whispered to Lulu and Anna. "Mimi and Rosalie will want to spend the whole day with us. They'll *beg.*"

"But we'll say *no,*" Lulu whispered back. "Agreed?"

Pam and Anna nodded.

Anna listened to Rosalie talking. "Okay," she told Mimi. "See you in a minute." Rosalie turned off the walkie-talkie and smiled at Anna. "Let's go get Mimi and Tongo."

Anna handed Acorn's reins to Lulu. Then she and Rosalie went across the town green to Mimi's house. Anna was surprised that Rosalie wasn't begging to go on the picnic.

When they walked into the Klines' backyard, Mimi was brushing Tongo.

"I'm getting Tongo ready," Mimi said. "This is going to be fun, fun, fun."

Why isn't Mimi begging to go on the picnic, either? Anna wondered.

Anna helped Mimi saddle Tongo. Mrs. Bell, Mimi's baby-sitter, came out the back door. She waved and called hello as she walked toward Anna. Mrs. Bell was carrying a wicker basket. Anna wondered what was in it.

"Anna," said Mrs. Bell, "you and your friends are so sweet and generous. I called Mimi's parents and Rosalie's mother. They all said that Rosalie and Mimi can join you for the trail ride and picnic."

"But . . ." Anna began.

"Thank you, Mrs. Bell," said Rosalie, interrupting Anna. "Thank you for calling my mother."

Anna didn't know what to say. Should she tell Mrs. Bell the girls couldn't go? Should she call the Klines and Mrs. Lacey? What would she say? "We don't really want to take your daughters on a picnic"?

Anna wished Lulu and Pam were there. They would know what to do.

"We're Junior Pony Pals," Mimi told Mrs. Bell. "So it's going to be a Pony Pal picnic."

Mrs. Bell took two lunch bags out of the wicker basket and handed them to Rosalie and Mimi. "I packed sandwiches for Mimi and Rosalie — I mean the Junior Pony Pals," she said. "And there are homemade chocolate cookies for all of you."

Anna stood there, speechless.

Mimi threw her arms around Anna. "Thank you," she said. "Thank you for letting us come on the ride and picnic."

Mrs. Bell gave Anna a tin box. "I put the cookies in here," she told Anna, "so they won't break during the ride."

"Good idea," said Anna.

The cookies might not break, thought Anna. But how am I going to *break* the news to Pam and Lulu? Rosalie, Mimi, and Tongo will be with us for the whole day!

Tongo nudged Anna. She turned and brushed his mane with her fingers. He was a cute pony.

"This is going to be so great," exclaimed Mimi.

Rosalie leaned her head against Tongo's neck. Rosalie loves ponies so much, thought Anna. And she's a good rider. It's too bad she can't ride more often.

"Don't worry, Anna," said Rosalie. "I won't beg to ride. I'll walk almost all the time."

Anna smiled at Rosalie. "It's okay," she said. "We'll take turns."

Mimi mounted Tongo and Anna led them across the town green. Rosalie walked beside Anna.

"*You* tell Lulu and Pam that you're coming on the picnic with us," Anna told Rosalie and Mimi.

Rosalie looked up at Anna. She had a worried look on her face. "Do you think they'll be mad?" she asked. "Because we tricked you."

"I don't think they'll be mad," answered Anna. "But they'll be surprised."

Crashing Water

Lulu and Pam were on their ponies at the gate to Pony Pal Trail.

"Guess what?" Mimi shouted to Lulu and Pam. "We can go on the picnic. Mrs. Bell said."

"But it wasn't Anna's fault," added Rosalie. "Mrs. Bell thought we were going on the picnic, too."

"I wonder where she got *that* idea," said Pam. She was staring right at Mimi when she said it.

"We'll be good," promised Rosalie. "It's going to be fun. *All* the Pony Pals together."

Mimi leaned over and hugged Tongo's neck. "You wanted to go on a picnic. Right, Tongo?"

Tongo nodded as if to say yes.

He looked so funny that everyone laughed. Maybe having Rosalie and Mimi along won't be so bad, thought Anna.

"You can ride Acorn for the first part," she told Rosalie.

"Yay!" shouted Rosalie. Anna handed her the reins and helped her mount.

"Let's go," said Pam. "I'll lead."

Rosalie pulled Acorn into line behind Pam and Lightning.

Anna led Mimi and Tongo behind Rosalie and Acorn.

Lulu and Snow White took up the rear.

The parade of girls and ponies rode through the gate and onto the trail.

Rosalie looked over her shoulder at Anna. "I love Pony Pal Trail rides," she said. "Thank you for letting me ride Acorn."

"You're welcome," replied Anna.

As Anna walked beside Tongo and Mimi, she remembered her own first trail rides. Riding on a trail is different from riding in the ring, thought Anna. On a trail ride, you're *going* somewhere.

Anna's very first trail ride was with Pam and her mother, Mrs. Crandal, who was a riding teacher. Anna took all her riding lessons from her. Pam's father, Dr. Crandal, was Acorn's veterinarian. Pam knew a lot about ponies. She was riding a pony before she learned to walk.

All the Pony Pals loved being outdoors with their ponies, especially in the woods around Wiggins.

Lulu Sanders knew the most about camping out and wild animals. Her father was a naturalist who traveled all over the world. Mr. Sanders studied and wrote about wild animals. Lulu's mother died when she was little. After that, Mr. Sanders took Lulu on his trips. When Lulu turned ten, her father said she should stay in one place for a while. Now Lulu lived with her grandmother in the house next to Anna's. That made it easy for Snow White and Acorn to be stable mates and for all the Pony Pals to be best friends.

Anna loved being a Pony Pal. She also loved drawing and painting. But she didn't like reading and writing that much. Anna was dyslexic, which made some schoolwork difficult for her.

Anna watched Rosalie riding Acorn. I'd rather ride than walk, she thought.

The trail widened and Lulu rode up beside Anna. "Do you want to ride Snow White for a while?" asked Lulu. "I'll walk."

Anna smiled up at her friend. Lulu had guessed what Anna was thinking. Anna loved it when that happened with her friends. "Thanks," she told Lulu. "Maybe later."

The trail narrowed again. Lulu and Snow White dropped back in line.

"Keep your heels down," Anna reminded Mimi.

"Let's use our walkie-talkies," Mimi shouted to Rosalie.

"Not while you're riding," Anna warned Mimi.

Mimi put both reins in one hand and dug into her pocket for her walkie-talkie. "It's okay," she said. "I can ride with one hand. See?"

"Mimi! Not while you're riding," repeated Anna.

Just then the walkie-talkie beeped. Tongo was startled by the noise. He turned suddenly and ran in the other direction.

Snow White whinnied as if to say, "Hey! Where's he going?"

"Hold on with two hands!" Lulu yelled to Mimi.

"Drop the walkie-talkie!" Anna shouted as she ran after the runaway pony.

The walkie-talkie flew through the air.

Pam halted Lightning.

Lulu jumped off Snow White.

Tongo raced down the trail.

Anna was terrified for Mimi. A branch could hit her. What if she fell off Tongo? What if he stepped on her by mistake?

"Stop, Tongo! Stop!" shouted Mimi.

"Keep your feet in the stirrups," yelled Anna. "Keep your head down."

Tongo was moving very fast.

Anna took a shortcut through the woods. She met Tongo and Mimi around the next turn in the trail. She reached out and grabbed Tongo's reins and he stopped.

By that time Mimi was half in and half out of the saddle.

"You get down," Anna told her. "I'll hold Tongo."

"Where's my walkie-talkie?" Mimi asked as she slid off her pony.

"Your walkie-talkie?" shouted Anna. "You almost got killed. You *have to* hold on with two hands when you ride. Always."

Pam came over to them. "Mimi, are you okay?" she asked.

"Sure," said Mimi. "That was fun. It was a Pony Pal adventure."

"Maybe we should take Mimi and Rosalie back right now," said Pam.

"You can have your picnic in your own backyard," added Anna.

"*No,*" wailed Mimi. "*Please.* I'll hold on with two hands. I promise."

"We're almost there," Lulu told Anna.

"Rosalie would be very disappointed if we turned back," added Anna.

"Me, too," said Mimi. "I'd be disappointed, too."

"Okay, Mimi," said Anna. "You can go on the picnic. But you have to do what I say."

"Okay," agreed Mimi.

"I'm leading you and Tongo the rest of the way," added Anna.

Rosalie handed Mimi her walkie-talkie. "It didn't break," she said.

"Good," said Mimi. "But we can't use them when we're riding." Mimi put the walkie-talkie in her pocket and grinned at Anna. "See," she said. "I'm being good."

The four riders and one walker continued their trail ride.

"We're getting near the waterfall," Anna

told Mimi and Rosalie. "Look how Acorn's ears are pointing forward. He loves the sound of the waterfall."

Lulu rode up beside Mimi and Tongo. "Snow White loves the waterfall, too," she told Mimi. "She likes to feel the cool spray."

Pam halted Lightning and turned in the saddle. "The trail is rough here," she said. "We'd better walk the rest of the way."

The girls led their ponies through the woods to the Badd Brook waterfall.

Suddenly, Tongo whinnied and reared up. Anna fell backward.

Pam rushed to calm down the little pony.

Anna scrambled to her feet. What's wrong with Tongo now? she wondered.

Hide-and-Seek

Pam held Tongo tightly by the reins. Lulu kept Rosalie and Mimi from going too close to him.

"It's okay, Tongo," Pam told the frightened pony. "Everything is okay."

"Maybe he got stung by a bee," suggested Lulu.

"Something spooked him," agreed Pam.

Tongo looked over his shoulder at the waterfall. Anna saw fear in his eyes. She put her hand on Tongo's neck. It was wet from the waterfall spray.

"Maybe he's spooked by the waterfall," Anna said. "He got sprayed."

Anna turned Tongo so he couldn't see the waterfall.

"Is Tongo afraid of water?" Lulu asked Mimi and Rosalie.

"He doesn't like sprinklers," said Rosalie. "Mr. Kline put on the big sprinkler that goes around and around. Tongo got sprayed by mistake. He was real scared."

"He doesn't like rain, either," said Mimi.

"Since he got spooked by the sprinkler," added Rosalie.

"We'd better not picnic here, then," said Lulu.

"We should help Tongo get over his fear," added Pam. "But not now."

"I'll take Tongo," said Anna. "Rosalie, will you lead Acorn for me?"

"Okay," agreed Rosalie.

Mimi ran up to Anna. "I want to ride Tongo," she said. "Please."

"Tongo's too upset now," said Anna. "We have to calm him down. We'll all walk."

Lulu and Anna exchanged a glance. Taking the Junior Pony Pals and Tongo on a trail ride and picnic was a lot of trouble.

After a ten-minute walk along Badd Brook, Pam stopped. The brook flowed calmly through a grassy field. There were big rocks at its edge. It was a perfect spot for a picnic.

Pam, Lulu, and Rosalie led the ponies to the brook to drink. Then they tied the ponies to trees.

Meanwhile, Anna and Mimi unpacked the picnic lunch and laid it out on a big rock.

Suddenly, Mimi's pocket beeped. Mimi grinned as she pulled out her walkie-talkie.

"Hi, Rosalie," Mimi said into the walkie-talkie.

"What are you doing?" asked Rosalie.

"I'm on a Pony Pal picnic," said Mimi.

The Pony Pals could hear both sides of the conversation without a walkie-talkie. Rosalie and Mimi were only a few feet away from each other.

"Let's eat," said Pam. "I'm hungry."

"Me, too," said Mimi and Rosalie together.

The five girls ate lunch and relaxed at the edge of the brook.

When they'd finished, Anna held up a roll of yellow string. "Let's play string games," she suggested. "Do you know how to do cat's cradle, Mimi?"

Mimi jumped to her feet. "Let's play with the walkie-talkies," she said.

Rosalie pointed across the field. "We're going over there," she explained.

Mimi handed Lulu her walkie-talkie. "You keep one walkie-talkie," she said, "and we'll take the other one."

Pam stood up and looked across the field. "Okay," she said. "But stay in the field where we can see you."

Rosalie and Mimi ran into the field. Anna and Lulu sat side by side on a rock with the walkie-talkie between them.

"Can you hear me?" Rosalie asked over the walkie-talkie.

"Yes," answered Anna. "I hear you loud and clear."

"Why did the chicken cross the road?" Mimi giggled.

"To get to the other side," Anna answered.

"Wrong!" screeched Mimi. "The chicken crossed the road to see her friend."

"Very funny," said Anna.

"Very *silly*," added Lulu.

"They're already at the end of the field," Pam told Anna and Lulu. "Tell them they should come back."

Lulu delivered Pam's message to the girls in the field. "Your walkie-talkie works great," she added.

"Why did the chicken throw the clock out the window?" asked Mimi.

"No more jokes," said Anna. "It's *time* to come back."

"Are they coming?" Lulu asked Pam.

"I can't see them anymore," answered Pam.

"Mimi, Rosalie, where are you?" Anna asked over the walkie-talkie. "We can't see you."

"You can't see us," Mimi said, "because we're hiding."

"We're playing walkie-talkie hide-and-seek," explained Rosalie. "This is how it works. We give you clues, and you see if you can find us."

"We're not playing hide-and-seek with you," said Anna. "You could get lost in the woods."

"We won't get lost," insisted Rosalie.

Lulu and Anna stood up, walked over to Pam, and looked out over the field, too. Pam was right. There was no sign of the two younger girls.

"We're not playing hide-and-seek with you," Anna repeated into the walkie-talkie. "Go back to the field. We *have to* be able to see you. We're supposed to be watching you two, remember? Especially Mimi."

"Please play with us," begged Mimi. "Please. Please. Please."

"Here's a clue," said Rosalie. "We're in the woods."

"What are we going to do?" Anna whispered to Pam. "They're not doing what we say."

"You can't find us. You can't find us," chanted Rosalie and Mimi over the walkie-talkie.

Tongo whinnied and pawed the ground.

"What's wrong with him now?" asked Lulu.

"You can't find us. You can't find us," repeated the younger girls.

Tongo looked around and whinnied again.

"I think he's confused," said Pam. "He can hear Mimi's voice, but he can't see her."

"Where are you?" Anna asked into the walkie-talkie.

"We can see everything, even Ms. Wiggins's house," said Rosalie. "We're on a big hill."

"Come find us," added Mimi.

"That sounds like Halpin's Hill," said Pam. "They couldn't have climbed up there so fast."

"They're fooling around," Lulu said. "And they're being big pains."

Anna felt annoyed at the younger girls. And at Tongo, too. They'd been nothing but trouble since the beginning of the trail ride.

What are we going to do? Anna wondered. How do we get Mimi and Rosalie to come back?

Cry Wolf!

"Let's look for Mimi and Rosalie in the field," suggested Lulu. "Maybe they're hiding in the grass. It's pretty tall."

"I'll stay here with the ponies," offered Pam.

Anna and Lulu walked into the field.

"Rosalie and Mimi," Lulu shouted into the walkie-talkie. "Come back. *Now!*"

"But we're lost!" said Mimi.

"Do you think they're *really* lost?" Lulu whispered to Anna.

"I don't know," answered Anna. "It's only been a little while, so they can't be too far away."

"If you are *really* lost," Lulu instructed the younger girls, "stop wherever you are. Then we can find you."

"We can't stop," said Mimi, "because a *bear* is chasing us."

"They're fooling around for sure," Anna whispered to Lulu.

"Okay, you two," Lulu said into the walkie-talkie. "Where are you?"

"We told you," said Mimi. "On a mountain. And Rosalie got hurt. When the bear chased us."

"This is nothing to fool around about," said Lulu in a stern voice.

"I have an idea," Anna told Lulu. "Let me talk to them."

Lulu handed Anna the walkie-talkie.

"Did you ever hear the story of the shepherd boy and the wolf?" Anna asked Mimi and Rosalie.

"What shepherd boy?" asked Mimi.

"There was this shepherd boy," began Anna, "from a long time ago. His job was to keep the sheep safe, especially from wolves. All day the shepherd was alone in the fields watching those sheep. He even slept in the fields at night. If he saw a wolf he was supposed to ring a big bell. Then the farmer would ride out to the field to catch the wolf and save the sheep."

While Anna told the story, she and Lulu searched for the girls in the tall grass. There was no sign of them.

"Is that the whole story?" asked Mimi over the walkie-talkie.

"There's more," continued Anna. "After a few days on the job, the boy was very lonely, so he *pretended* there was a wolf. He rang the bell with all his might and hollered, 'Wolf! Wolf!' The farmer and two other men came on horseback.

" 'Where's the wolf?' asked the farmer.

" 'I saw him,' said the boy. He pointed to some bushes. 'Over there.' "

"He told a *lie*," said Rosalie.

"It wasn't a lie," said Mimi. "He was *joking*."

"The farmer stayed for a long time waiting for that wolf," continued Anna. "The boy was happy because he had company. After that, whenever the boy was lonely, he'd ring the bell and holler, 'Wolf! Wolf!' Finally, the farmer figured out that there was no wolf."

"Did that shepherd boy get punished?" asked Rosalie.

"Listen to what happened next," said Anna. "One day the boy really did see a wolf. He rang the bell long and hard. But the farmer didn't believe the boy anymore. So he didn't come, and the wolf killed one of the sheep."

"Did the wolf kill the boy, too?" asked Mimi.

"I don't know," answered Anna. "Maybe."

"So you see," said Lulu, "it's dangerous to *pretend* you're in trouble. Then no one will believe you when you *are* in trouble."

"That's so funny you told us that story," Rosalie said over the walkie-talkie. "Because we *just* saw a wolf. Right, Mimi?"

"A big bad wolf," said Mimi. "Like the one in 'Little Red Riding Hood.' "

"If you don't stop fooling around, I'm turning off the walkie-talkie," Anna told Rosalie and Mimi. "Do you understand?"

"What about the *wolf*?" asked Mimi. "We're scared it might *eat* us." Rosalie giggled in the background.

"Over and out," said Anna. She turned off the walkie-talkie.

Anna and Lulu ran back to the picnic site.

Pam was feeding carrots to the ponies. She looked up at her friends. "Where are Rosalie and Mimi?" she asked.

"They're hiding," answered Lulu.

"So what do we do now?" asked Anna.

"Don't pay any attention to them," said Pam. "Then they'll stop being silly and come back."

"They'll get bored," added Lulu. "I'm surprised at Rosalie. She should know better."

"But she's with Mimi," Pam put in. "Sometimes Rosalie acts younger when she's with Mimi."

The walkie-talkie beeped.

"Let me talk to them," said Pam.

Anna handed her the walkie-talkie.

"There are more wolves," screeched Mimi. "They're surrounding us."

"Listen up, Rosalie and Mimi," said Pam in a stern voice. "We're not playing this game with you. It's time to come back. Do you understand?"

Anna leaned over Pam to speak into the walkie-talkie. "We'll still hang out with you guys this afternoon," she said. "Just come back."

"But no more fooling around," added Lulu.

The Pony Pals heard Mimi tell Rosalie, "They're so *bossy*."

Pam turned off the walkie-talkie.

"I wonder where they are," said Anna.

Anna looked up at the sky to think about

what to do. In the distance she saw big dark clouds moving quickly toward them.

She pointed to the sky. "Look at the clouds," she said.

"Those are storm clouds," said Lulu. "And they're headed this way."

5

The Runaway

Anna took the walkie-talkie from Pam and beeped the girls. "Rosalie and Mimi," she said. "There's a big storm headed this way. Come back. We have to go home right away."

"It might *snow*, too," joked Rosalie.

"I'm serious," said Anna. She was angry.

"That storm is definitely coming this way," said Lulu.

"But Mimi and Rosalie don't believe us," Anna said. "They think it's a big joke."

Anna looked at the big clouds moving toward them. In the far distance she saw a quick flash of lightning.

How can we convince them to come back? wondered Anna. A lightning storm could be very dangerous.

The thunder rumbled again. This time it was louder and closer. Anna wondered if Rosalie and Mimi heard it.

Tongo heard it. He whinnied fearfully.

Pam held Tongo by a tight rein. To calm him down, she walked him in a circle. But he was still upset.

The sky above them darkened with storm clouds. It was becoming colder and windier by the second.

Snow White nickered and pawed the ground. Lightning snorted. Tongo is making Snow White and Lightning nervous, thought Anna. She was glad that Acorn wasn't upset.

Anna took her rain jacket out of the saddlebag and put it on. As soon as she snapped the last snap, it started to rain. Within a few seconds the drops were falling hard and fast.

Anna turned on the walkie-talkie. "Mimi, Rosalie, can you hear me?" she asked. "Are you all right? It's time to tell us where you are," she added firmly.

There was no answer.

"I can't reach them," Anna told her friends.

"Maybe they're out of range," suggested Lulu.

"Or they're still fooling around," said Pam.

The rain slapped against Anna's face. She tied the hood on her rain jacket. "Mimi is afraid of thunder and lightning," said Anna. "I was at her house once during a thunder-storm. She got really scared."

Anna held the walkie-talkie out to Pam. "You try to talk to them," she said.

Pam reached for the walkie-talkie.

Tongo pulled back suddenly and ran across the field.

"I'll get him!" shouted Anna as she ran after Tongo. But the little pony was fast. Soon he was in the woods and out of sight.

"Anna, come back!" Lulu and Pam shouted after her.

Anna wanted to go into the woods and look for Tongo. But Pam and Lulu were calling her. They're right, Anna thought. I can't go after Tongo. We have to find Mimi and Rosalie. Right now that's more important than finding Tongo.

Anna turned around and went back to her friends.

"It's time for an emergency Pony Pal meeting," Lulu said. "I think Mimi and Rosalie might really be lost. We're going to have to do a search."

"It's going to be hard to find them in this storm," said Anna.

"We'll have to keep our ponies with us," said Pam.

"Which could slow us down in the woods," added Lulu.

"Maybe we should split up for the search," suggested Anna.

"I can search alone," said Lulu. "I know these woods pretty well."

"You *are* the best tracker," added Pam.

"We'll keep Snow White with us so you can move faster," said Anna.

"Okay," agreed Lulu. She untied Snow White's lead rope and handed it to Anna.

"Let's decide on whistle signals," said Anna.

"Two long whistle blasts mean we found Mimi and Rosalie," suggested Pam. "One long blast says we found Tongo. Two short blasts mean we heard the signal."

"And short–long–short is SOS," added Anna.

Lulu pulled her whistle on over her head. Next, she took a bottle of water and her flashlight from her saddlebag. "Do you have the first-aid kit?" she asked Pam.

"Yes," answered Pam. "I just hope we don't have to use it."

"Me, too," said Lulu. "See you later."

Lulu ran across the field toward the woods.

It was still raining hard.

Acorn shook the water from his mane and

whinnied as if to say, "Why are we standing around in the rain?"

"We're going to search for Mimi and Rosalie," Anna told Acorn.

The two girls led the ponies across the wet field.

"I really wish Rosalie and Mimi would call us on the walkie-talkie," said Anna.

"Do you think they're still fooling around?" asked Pam.

"I hope not," answered Anna. "They could be lost and not even know it."

"They must be so cold and wet," said Pam.

"And if they're lost, they must be frightened," added Anna.

Anna felt frightened, too. What if they couldn't find the two lost girls in the storm?

"I Can't Hear You!"

Anna and Pam led the three ponies onto the trail. "I just hope Rosalie and Mimi stuck to the trail," said Anna.

"Look for clues," suggested Pam. "Maybe they dropped something. Or we'll find a footprint."

Suddenly, the walkie-talkie beeped. Pam took it out of her pocket and spoke into it.

"Rosalie, Mimi," she said. "We're in the woods. We're looking for you."

She held up the walkie-talkie so Anna could talk into it, too.

"Where are you?" Anna asked. "Are you all right?"

"We're in a cave," said the voice over the walkie-talkie. It was Rosalie's voice.

"It's not raining in the cave, Anna," said Mimi. "But it's really dark."

"We came in here to get out of the rain," added Rosalie.

"If this is a joke," said Anna sternly, "it is a really *bad* one."

"It's true," said Mimi.

"Please believe us," pleaded Rosalie. "We're not like the shepherd boy."

"Where is the cave?" asked Pam. "Tell us."

"I don't know," said Rosalie. "We ran and ran. We got lost in the woods."

Anna and Pam exchanged a glance. They both believed the girls were telling the truth.

"Listen carefully," said Pam. "Get out of the cave. Then we can find you."

"It's dark in here," said Mimi. Her voice was shaking with fear.

Anna held the walkie-talkie to her ear. She

could hear Mimi and Rosalie talking to each other.

"I'm scared," said Mimi.

"Don't worry, Mimi," Rosalie said. "The Pony Pals will help us. They'll save us."

It's my fault that they're lost, thought Anna. I shouldn't have let them come on the ride.

"This is serious," Pam whispered to Anna. "Really serious. How are we going to find them in a cave?"

Acorn pulled on his lead rope. Then he butted Anna with his head. She almost dropped the walkie-talkie.

"Acorn, stop it," Anna scolded.

Acorn pulled on his lead rope again.

I don't have time to figure out what's bothering Acorn, thought Anna. I have to help Mimi and Rosalie.

"Stay calm," Anna said into the walkie-talkie. "Where did you go into the woods?"

"Anna, are you there?" asked Rosalie.

"Where did you go into the woods?" Anna

repeated loudly. The lost girls still didn't answer her question.

"I don't think they can hear me," Anna told Pam.

"How did you find the cave?" Pam asked into the walkie-talkie.

"We're lost," said Rosalie.

Rosalie didn't answer Pam's question, either, thought Anna.

"Were you on a trail before you went into the cave?" Pam asked loudly.

"Please talk to us," said Rosalie.

"They can't hear us," Pam told Anna.

"Here. Let me try again," said Anna.

Rosalie's voice came over the walkie-talkie. "How come you guys aren't talking to us?" she asked.

"We are talking to you," said Anna.

"Please talk to us," said Rosalie. "We're sorry we joked. But this is true. We're really in a cave and we can't get out. It's dark."

Anna heard Mimi crying in the background.

"Something's wrong with our walkie-talkie," Anna told Pam. "They can't hear us."

"But we can hear them," said Pam. "So it's not all broken. It works one way."

"They must be so scared," said Anna.

Anna was thinking about what to do next, when Acorn got away from her.

Snow White whinnied as if to say, "Hey! Where are you going?"

Pam held Lightning tightly so she wouldn't follow Acorn.

"Acorn!" yelled Anna as she ran along the trail after him. In the distance she saw a smaller, golden-colored pony. Tongo, thought Anna. Acorn saw Tongo and is running after him. Both ponies were moving fast. Anna knew that she couldn't catch up to them.

She ran back and told Pam that she had seen Tongo. And that Acorn had seen him, too.

"Now two ponies are missing, our walkie-talkie isn't working, and Mimi and Rosalie are in a cave," said Pam.

"We'd better tell Lulu all those things," said Anna.

Pam nodded.

Anna raised her whistle to her mouth and blew. Short–long–short.

Two short blasts answered the SOS. Lulu had heard the signal and she wasn't very far away.

Snow White whinnied. Anna recognized that whinny. It was how Snow White greeted Lulu. A minute later, Lulu came out of the woods.

"Snow White knew you were coming," Anna told her.

Lulu brushed the rainwater off her pony's side. "She's a good pony," she said. Lulu looked around. "Where's Acorn?" she asked.

The Missing Four

"Acorn ran off," Pam told Lulu. "He saw Tongo and went after him."

"Maybe Acorn will bring Tongo back to us," said Lulu.

"I hope so," said Anna.

Anna was already upset about Mimi and Rosalie. And now her pony was missing, too.

"Is that why you sent the SOS?" asked Lulu. "Because of Acorn?"

"No," answered Pam. "Mimi and Rosalie got through to us. They went in a cave to get out of the rain. But we don't know where the cave is. And now our walkie-talkie isn't working."

"There are a lot of caves around here," commented Lulu.

"Did you find any clues about which way they went?" Anna asked her.

"Not one," answered Lulu.

"It's going to be hard to find them without the walkie-talkie," said Pam.

"Maybe the walkie-talkie doesn't work because they're in a cave," said Lulu. "And it will work when they come out."

"We can hear them," said Anna. "I think something's wrong with *this* walkie-talkie."

Anna pushed the hood back on her rain jacket. It had finally stopped raining. The three friends huddled around the walkie-talkie.

It beeped again, and they heard Rosalie's sad and frightened voice. "Why won't you talk to us?" she asked.

"Can you hear us now?" asked Anna back.

"Please talk to us," begged Mimi.

Anna handed the walkie-talkie to Lulu. "What's wrong with this thing?" she asked.

"Maybe the batteries are weak," Lulu suggested. "Let me see it."

Lulu opened the battery case and took out the two batteries. "These are the same type of batteries as the ones in our flashlight," she said.

"Let's switch batteries," suggested Anna.

"It's worth a try," said Lulu.

Anna got the flashlight out of Snow White's saddlebag. She unscrewed the top, took out the batteries, and put them in the walkie-talkie. Lulu closed the battery cover case.

Meanwhile, Anna put the walkie-talkie batteries in the flashlight. She turned on the flashlight. It didn't work.

Lulu pressed the beeper button and spoke into the walkie-talkie. "Mimi, Rosalie, can you hear me?" she asked.

"Yes!" came the answer over the walkie-talkie.

Lulu told Mimi and Rosalie that they'd had trouble with the walkie-talkie. "But it's working now," said Lulu. "Are you out of the cave?"

"No," wailed Mimi. "We're lost. *Really!*"

"We tried to get out," said Rosalie. "But we got even more lost."

The Pony Pals exchanged a glance. Rosalie and Mimi were alone and *lost* in a dark cave. They didn't have sweaters, a flashlight, water, or food. The situation was even more serious than they had thought.

"It's dark in here," cried Mimi.

"Try to stay calm," Pam told the girls. "We'll find you. But we need your help."

"Describe everything you remember *before* you went in the cave," instructed Lulu.

"We were in the woods so you couldn't see us," said Mimi. "And we climbed a big hill."

"Outside the cave there was a big rock," added Rosalie. "The cave is behind the rock."

"Did you cross the brook?" asked Lulu.

"Yes," answered Rosalie. "We walked on some rocks."

"Was the brook wide where you went across?" asked Lulu.

"No," answered Rosalie.

Anna leaned over to whisper to Pam. "What if *their* walkie-talkie batteries wear out?" she said.

When Lulu finished interviewing the girls, she handed the walkie-talkie to Anna.

"We aren't going to talk to you a lot," Anna told the lost girls. "We all have to save battery power. But we're going to find you. Okay?"

"Okay," agreed Rosalie.

"Anna, can I talk to Tongo?" asked Mimi. Pam and Anna exchanged a glance. If Mimi knew Tongo was missing she'd get even more upset.

"Tongo is busy right now," Anna told Mimi. "He's looking for you, too."

"We're going to start our search now," Pam said into the walkie-talkie. "Stay where you are. We will find you. We'll beep you if we need to talk."

"Okay," said Rosalie. "Over and out."

Anna knew that Rosalie was trying to be brave. But she could hear the fear in her voice.

Pam looked at Lulu and Anna. "How are we going to find them?" she asked.

"First I'm going to write down what they told me," said Lulu. "Those are our clues."

Pam took her notebook and a pencil out of her pocket and handed them to Lulu.

Lulu flipped opened the notebook and wrote:

Went through woods to trail
Crossed a narrow part of Badd Brook
Many rocks in brook for walking across
Climbed a big hill
Cave entrance behind a big rock

The Pony Pals studied Lulu's notes.

"There are a lot of trails around here," said Pam. "And hills."

"And caves behind big rocks," added Anna.

"And Badd Brook is narrow in many places," said Lulu.

Anna felt her heart sink.

How would they ever find the right cave?

Batteries Required

Suddenly, a loud whinny startled Anna. She turned around and saw Acorn coming toward her along the trail. But Tongo wasn't with him.

Anna ran to meet Acorn. She grabbed his lead rope. Acorn shook his head. He didn't want Anna to hold on to him.

"Now, settle down, Acorn," Anna said softly.

Pam and Lulu came up beside Anna.

"Where's Tongo?" asked Pam.

"He's not here," said Anna.

Acorn pulled on the lead rope by jerking his head.

"Why is he doing that?" asked Lulu.

"I think he wants to show me something," answered Anna.

"Maybe he'll lead us to Mimi and Rosalie," said Lulu.

"Let's try following him for a little while," suggested Anna.

"It's worth a try," agreed Lulu. She held up the notebook. "We'll look for the places Rosalie described."

Lulu and Pam went back for their ponies. Anna let go of Acorn's lead rope. "Go ahead, Acorn," she said. Acorn turned and ran along the trail while Anna raced to keep up with him.

Soon Pam and Lulu rode up on their ponies.

Acorn suddenly turned off the trail.

Lulu and Pam dismounted. The three girls and the two ponies followed Acorn as he pushed past bushes and went into the woods.

"I hope he knows what he's doing," mumbled Pam.

"He acts like he does," said Lulu.

Acorn led them onto a narrow trail.

"I found a clue," shouted Lulu excitedly. "A footprint. Over here in the mud."

Anna grabbed Acorn's lead rope to stop him. "Wait a minute, Acorn," she said.

As Lulu pointed, Anna bent over and studied the clear print of a small riding boot.

"Mimi has on riding boots," Anna told Lulu.

"They must have come this way, then," concluded Pam.

Pam beeped the girls in the cave. She told them that Acorn had picked up their trail.

"Hurry," said Rosalie. "It's really scary in here."

"Talk to us some more," pleaded Mimi.

"It's time to turn off the walkie-talkie," Pam told her. "So you don't use up the batteries. Remember?"

"Okay," said Rosalie. "Over and out."

Lulu stopped at another spot on the trail. "I think Tongo came this way," she said.

Anna saw Lulu's second clue — a small pony's hoofprints in the mud.

"So we're following Tongo, too," said Anna. "Good work, Acorn." Anna patted her pony's head.

The search party continued to follow Acorn. Finally, he led them out of the dense woods to the edge of Badd Brook.

"Acorn brought us to the brook," Anna shouted back to her friends.

Lulu and Pam and their ponies came up beside Anna and Acorn. They faced a narrow section of Badd Brook. There were many big rocks for crossing.

Lulu looked at her notes. " 'Crossed a narrow part of Badd Brook,' " she read. " 'Many rocks in brook for walking across.' "

"This must be the place Rosalie described," said Pam. She beeped the girls again. "We're crossing the brook," she told them. "There's a hill on the other side."

The Pony Pals and their ponies crossed the brook.

As Anna walked up the steep hill beside Acorn, she thought of Mimi and Rosalie.

Rosalie had said they were in total darkness. A shudder ran through Anna. She, too, was afraid of small dark spaces. Being lost in a dark cave was the scariest thing she could imagine.

Acorn stopped suddenly, raised his head, and nickered loudly. Then a nicker answered him.

"It's Tongo!" exclaimed Pam.

Halfway up the hill, Acorn made a right turn past some trees. Anna looked ahead and saw Tongo standing in front of a big rock. He was waiting for them. Acorn ran ahead to Tongo.

"Come on," Anna shouted to Lulu and Pam. "We found Tongo."

The three girls and four ponies gathered around the big rock. Lulu looked at her notes and read, " 'Cave entrance behind a big rock.' "

"I think I just figured something out," Anna told her friends.

"What?" asked Lulu and Pam together.

"Maybe Tongo ran away to find Mimi and Rosalie," she said. "Not because he was afraid of the storm."

"And Acorn followed Tongo," added Lulu. "Then he came to get us."

"Beep Mimi and Rosalie," Lulu told Pam. "Tell them where we are." She looked up at the rocky hillside behind the rock. "I bet the cave is in this hill someplace."

Anna looked up at the hill, too. Were the two lost girls somewhere inside that hill? Could the Pony Pals get them out without getting lost themselves?

Angel Rock

The Pony Pals went behind the big rock and looked up at the steep hill. They didn't see an entrance to a cave anywhere.

Pam beeped Rosalie and Mimi on the walkie-talkie. "We're standing at a big rock."

"Ask Rosalie to describe the rock near the cave," suggested Lulu.

"What does the big rock near the cave look like?" Anna asked into the walkie-talkie. "Did you notice?"

"The rock looks like an angel," answered Rosalie. "It has wings."

"I asked the angel rock to take care of us," said Rosalie. Anna heard tears in Rosalie's voice.

"It's all right, Rosalie," Anna said into the walkie-talkie. "We found the rock and now we're going to find you."

"You're being very brave," added Pam, "and you'll be out of the cave very soon."

Anna felt tears in her own eyes. She wondered how much longer Rosalie and Mimi would be lost inside the cave.

Lulu and Anna stepped back for a better view of the rock. The rock was high and narrow. Two sections of the rock stuck out — like wings.

"This rock does look like an angel," said Anna.

"But I don't see an entrance to a cave," Lulu whispered to Anna and Pam.

"How did you get into the cave?" Pam asked Rosalie. "Was there anything special about the entrance?"

"It's behind a tree," answered Rosalie. "It's

little. We crawled in, and then we couldn't see how to get out."

"Stay right where you are," Pam said. "Okay?"

"Okay," answered Rosalie.

Lulu pointed to her right. "I'll look for the cave over there," she told Anna. She pointed to the left. "You look in that direction."

Anna walked behind a couple of the trees. She didn't find anything, though.

"I think I found it!" Lulu shouted from behind a big pine tree.

Anna and Pam went over to Lulu. She was crouched on the ground, facing a small opening in the rock ledge.

Anna knelt beside Lulu and looked into the cave. Her heart beat faster. Just looking into the cave made her nervous.

"It's bigger inside," she told Lulu and Pam.

"But that opening is so small," said Lulu.

"I bet that's why they got lost," Anna said as she stood up. "The opening is so small they couldn't find it to get out."

"It's very dark in there," added Lulu.

"Okay," Pam said into the walkie-talkie. "We found the cave. Now we're going to come after you."

"There's not a lot of room in there," Lulu told Anna and Pam. "It's better if only one person goes in."

Rosalie and Mimi are a lot smaller than Pam and Lulu, thought Anna. And so am I. I'm scared, but I'm still the best Pony Pal to go into the cave.

"I'll do it," Anna told Lulu and Pam. "I'll go after them."

"Are you sure?" said Lulu. "I could try."

"I'm the smallest," Anna told her. "So it should be me."

Pam looked from the entrance to the cave to Anna. "Okay," she agreed. "But how are you going to find them?"

"She needs the flashlight," said Lulu. "We'll have to take the batteries out of the walkie-talkie and put them back in the flashlight."

"But what if Mimi and Rosalie can't hear

me in the cave?" protested Anna. "I might need the walkie-talkie."

"You have to choose between having a flashlight or having a walkie-talkie," said Lulu.

Anna thought about the darkness of the cave. "I choose the flashlight," she said. She held up her whistle. "I can signal them with my whistle. If they yell back, it will help me find them."

"Anna's coming in after you," Pam told Rosalie and Mimi. "She'll have a flashlight, so look for a beam of light. And she'll blow her whistle. When you hear the whistle, start shouting."

"I'm coming in right now," Anna shouted toward the walkie-talkie.

Lulu took the walkie-talkie and spoke to the girls, too. "I have to take the batteries out of the walkie-talkie now," she said. "Anna needs them for the flashlight."

"Okay," agreed Rosalie.

"Hurry up," added Mimi.

Lulu turned off the walkie-talkie and took

out the batteries. She put them in the flashlight and handed it to Anna.

Anna knelt down in front of the cave. It was time to crawl inside. Anna was very frightened. *What if I get lost in there, too?* she thought.

Anna stuck her head and one arm in the cave entrance.

"Anna! Wait!" shouted Lulu. "I have an idea."

Anna backed out of the cave and looked up at Lulu. Lulu was holding up the ball of yellow string. It was the string Anna had brought for playing string games with Mimi and Rosalie.

Anna and Lulu smiled at each other. Anna knew what Lulu's idea was. So did Pam.

"That's a great idea, Lulu," said Anna.

"I'll hold the end," Lulu told Anna. "You unroll the rest behind you."

"Then when it's time to come out," added Pam, "you follow the yellow string back to us."

"We'll be connected the whole time," said Lulu.

If the string is long enough, thought Anna.

Lulu sat by the cave entrance. She held the end of the string and handed the ball to Anna.

Anna put her head and her arms back in the cave. Then she pulled in her legs, one after the other. The earth felt damp and cold on her hands and knees. She turned on the flashlight and looked around. There was no room to stand up. She would have to crawl to find the girls.

After going forward a few feet, Anna looked behind her. She couldn't see the entrance to the cave anymore. It had disappeared in the darkness. Anna beamed the flashlight around until she found the yellow string behind her. She followed it with the flashlight until she saw the entrance.

Lulu stuck her head into the cave. "Are you all right in there?" she shouted.

"I'm okay," Anna yelled back.

"Don't forget to use the SOS whistle signal if you need help," said Lulu.

I can do this, Anna told herself. I can find the girls. I have a flashlight and a whistle. And Lulu has the other end of the string.

Anna beamed the flashlight around the cave. Where should I begin to look for Rosalie and Mimi? she wondered.

My Hero

Anna blew a long blast on her whistle. The sound echoed deep inside the cave. She listened for an answer. But she heard nothing.

Anna beamed the flashlight around the cave again. She kept the beam of light close to the ground. Finally, she saw an opening in the rock wall of the cave room.

It looks just like the entrance I came in, thought Anna. No wonder Rosalie and Mimi got lost.

Anna crawled carefully toward the opening. She trailed the string behind her. When she reached the opening, she crawled through it.

Anna beamed her light around the second cave room. The girls weren't in there. She noticed that the second cave room was larger than the first space. But she still couldn't stand up.

Suddenly, the beam from the flashlight flickered and weakened.

Anna's heart thumped in her chest. What if the batteries died on her now? How would she find the girls without a flashlight?

I have to save the batteries, thought Anna. She turned the flashlight off. She squeezed the ball of string. How far will this string go? she wondered. In the dark she felt for the whistle around her neck. When she found it, she blew as hard as she could. Then she sat back on her heels and listened for an answer.

Anna thought she heard shouts in the distance. They were coming from her right.

Anna pointed the flashlight in the direction of the shouts and turned it back on for a second. In the weak beam of light Anna saw an opening in the rock wall.

"I hear you," Anna shouted. "I'm coming to get you."

She turned off the flashlight and crawled on her hands and knees across the cave room floor.

Suddenly, her head hit the hard side of the cave. "Ouch!" she shouted.

"Ouch!" came her echo. The cave was bigger than she'd imagined. The girls could be very far away.

Anna felt very scared again. Two things were going wrong. The batteries on the flashlight were dying. And the string was running out.

Anna turned the flashlight on for an instant. The dying beam showed her the hole in the rock wall. She quickly crawled over to it and beamed the light through.

"We see the light!" a voice shouted. It was Rosalie's voice.

"Anna! Anna!" shouted Mimi.

"Don't move," Anna shouted into the

hole. "Stay right where you are."

Anna turned off the flashlight again.

"Anna, where'd you go?" shouted Rosalie.

"We're here. We're in here," cried Mimi.

"I'm still here," Anna shouted. "I'm coming in." Anna crawled through the hole and turned the flashlight back on. Please work, Anna prayed. It did, but the beam of light was even weaker than before.

Anna quickly moved the beam around the cave room.

"Here we are!" shouted Mimi.

Anna finally saw the two girls. They were huddled together in a corner of the cave room. It was the biggest of the three rooms Anna had seen.

Anna turned off the light.

"What happened?" shouted Rosalie.

"Where'd you go?" asked Mimi.

"I saw you," Anna shouted into the dark. "Now do exactly what I say. When I put the flashlight back on, crawl across the cave to me. Follow the light. The batteries are dying, so hurry. Okay?"

"Okay," answered Rosalie and Mimi in unison.

Anna turned on the flashlight again. She watched the two little girls crawling toward her. As they came closer, the beam of light became weaker. By the time Mimi and Rosalie reached Anna, the light had died completely.

They were in total darkness again.

"Anna," whispered Mimi, "please turn the light back on. I'm still so scared."

Anna reached for Mimi's hand in the dark and squeezed it. "I can't," she told the little girl. "The batteries died. But don't worry. You're safe now. I know how to get out of here."

"How?" asked Rosalie. "It's so dark."

Anna told them about the string. "We're going to crawl out like a train," she explained. "It's the safest way. I'll tie my jacket to my foot. You both hold on to it. We'll follow the string."

Anna tied one arm of her jacket to her foot.

"Mimi, you go behind Anna," said Rosalie bravely. "I'll be last."

Anna crawled through the hole into the second room. She reached back and helped both of the girls through.

"We're going to move slowly," Anna said. "That way, no one will get hurt. And we'll keep talking. That will help us stay together and be brave."

Anna felt the floor of the second cave room for the string. When she found it she crawled along it. Mimi held on to Anna's jacket and crawled behind her.

"Don't pull on the jacket when I'm crawling," Anna warned. "Or I'll fall on my face."

"Okay," Mimi agreed.

Anna knew that this time Mimi would do exactly what she was told.

After a few minutes of crawling through the second room, Anna's head hit a rock wall again. "Everybody stop," she told Mimi and Rosalie.

Anna felt around for the opening to the first room. When she found it she went through. Then she helped the girls. "We're in the first cave room now," she said in the dark. "We're almost out."

Anna crawled more quickly along the string now.

"Lulu, Pam," Anna shouted, "we're coming out!"

"Yay!" Lulu shouted.

Anna felt a little tug on the string. She tugged back.

Finally, Anna reached the entrance to the first cave room. She moved aside and helped Mimi out of the cave and into the light. Rosalie crawled out behind Mimi, and Anna crawled out last.

Rosalie and Mimi blinked in the bright sunlight. Lulu hugged the little girls.

Pam handed them boxes of juice. "You're safe," she said. "You're all safe."

Everyone was crying with happiness and relief.

Tongo came over to Mimi and sniffed at her. "We were lost," Mimi told her pony.

"First, you hid on us," said Pam.

"We thought it would be fun," said Rosalie. "It was for a little while."

"It was never fun for us," Lulu told her. "We were afraid you'd get lost or hurt."

"We did get lost," admitted Mimi.

"But we didn't know we were lost until we tried to come back," added Rosalie. "Then it rained and we went into the cave. That was a big mistake."

Mimi smiled. "But the Pony Pals saved us," she said.

"Tongo and Acorn saved you, too," Anna told Mimi. "Tongo ran away from us to look for you. He found the angel rock. Acorn led us to Tongo and the rock."

Acorn whinnied as if to say, "That's right."

"Tongo's a hero!" exclaimed Mimi. "*My* pony's a hero."

Anna gave Acorn a big hug. "You're my hero, Acorn," she whispered in his ear. "My wonderful pony hero."

Dear Reader,

I am having fun researching and writing the Pony Pal books. I've met great kids and wonderful ponies at homes, farms, and riding schools. Some of my ideas for Pony Pal adventures have even come from these visits!

I remember the day I made up the main characters for the series. I was walking on a country road in New England. First, I decided that the three girls would be smart, independent, and kind. Then I gave them their names—Pam, Anna, and Lulu. (Look at the initial of each girl's name. See what it spells when you put them together!) Later, I created the three ponies. When I reached home, I turned on my computer and started to write. And I haven't stopped since!

My friends say that I am a little bit like all of the Pony Pals. I am very organized, like Pam. I love nature, like Lulu. But I think that I am most like Anna. I am dyslexic and a good artist, just like her.

Readers often wonder about my life. I live in an apartment in New York City near Central Park and the Museum of Natural History. I enjoy swimming, hiking, painting, and reading. I also love to make up stories. I have been writing novels for children and young adults for more than twenty years! Several of my books have won the Children's Choice Award.

Many Pony Pal readers send me letters, drawings, and photos. I tape them to the wall in my office. They inspire me to write more Pony Pal stories. Thank you very much!

I don't ride anymore and I've never had a pony. But you don't have to ride to love ponies! And you certainly don't need a pony to be a Pony Pal.

Happy Reading,

Jeanne Betancourt